AF094319

A Little Love, A Little Laughter
Torn pages from the book of life

Swapna Dutta

Ukiyoto Publishing

All global publishing rights are held by

Ukiyoto Publishing

Published in 2023

Content Copyright © Swapna Dutta

ISBN 9789360160630

All rights reserved.

No part of this publication may be reproduced, transmitted, or stored in a retrieval system, in any form by any means, electronic, mechanical, photocopying, recording or otherwise, without the prior permission of the publisher.

The moral rights of the author have been asserted.

This is a work of fiction. Names, characters, businesses, places, events, locales, and incidents are either the products of the author's imagination or used in a fictitious manner. Any resemblance to actual persons, living or dead, or actual events is purely coincidental.

This book is sold subject to the condition that it shall not by way of trade or otherwise, be lent, resold, hired out or otherwise circulated, without the publisher's prior consent, in any form of binding or cover other than that in which it is published.

www.ukiyoto.com

Dedication and Acknowledgements

This book is dedicated with love to those of my Facebook friends who enjoyed my "middles" and Facebook postings over the years and wanted me to put them together in a book.

All the incidents described in this book appeared as "Middles" or "Humour" pieces in various newspapers, including The Times of India, Hindustan Times, Indian Express, The Statesman, The Pioneer, Readers' Digest, Deccan Herald and Sunday Herald. The rest appeared as postings on Facebook.

Foreword

I feel that there are moments and incidents in everyone's life that are hilarious, absurd and diverting enough to entertain the reader. Or else make them pause, think and remember something similar that happened to them. Incidents that could make someone ponder over an issue or simply enjoy the joke. Or read about a time that is quite different from now.That's the sort of memories I have been sharing in my newspaper "middles" and my Facebook postings over the years. And of course I have woven many of them into my stories. Life is serious, sometimes worrisome and often complicated where a breather is usually welcome. This book is meant for all who enjoy such breaks.

I have divided the contents into three parts. *Salad Days* deal with incidents belonging to my school, college and university days. What happened when we wanted to buy English records for our common room? Or had our letters censored by the superintendent of the college hostel?I have also described my first job in college in a small and conservative town that by and large did not believe in higher studies for women. How did we go about collecting students? *Learning to Be a Housewife* deals with the next chapter of my life where hilarious mistakes of every kind happened. Was it easy to face the fish-seller, the vet or the prying neighbours?*And That is Life* has incidents and musings right up to my twilight years, many of them about a different time and place, all of them diverting in their own way. What I have really come to realize over the years is the fact that Life never stops surprising you.

This book is dedicated with love to all those of my Facebook friends who have enjoyed my postings over the years and wanted me to put the pieces together in a book.

Contents

Salad Days	1
Learning To Be A Housewife	33
And …. ThatIs Life!	58
About the Author	*87*

Salad Days

Just For the Record

Although our college had a beautiful and impressive building our Common Room was rather small in comparison. Nevertheless it had one attraction. There was an ancient record player and some really nice records which all of us had access to. So although we preferred to spend our free periods in the vast college garden we dropped in there every now and then to enjoy our favourite songs. But most of the records were in Bengali. There were very few English ones. I was a student of the first year but my friend and I knew a few seniors who also loved English songs. We asked them if they couldn't do something about it. Sarah, who was one of the shining lights of the third year, took up our cause and got the Department of Culture to permit us to go and buy some 'suitable' English records for the Common Room. Incidentally, those were the days of 78 rpm records. CDs had not yet come in and Extended and Long Playing records were too expensive for the common man. Luckily there was a record shop virtually next door to our college and we got permission to go there for our shopping. There were just eight of us – six from the Third year and two of us from the First.

The shop was dark and tiny. As we looked around it seemed at first that they stocked only Bengali records. But Roma, an avid pop music fan, located a pile in a corner of the shelf which had some of the latest favourites – Elvis Presley, Pat Boone, Tony Brent, Doris Day, Connie Francis, among others. She let out a wild yell, startling the owner of the shop and an elderly crony who was visiting him, who frowned in intense disapproval. The young salesman grinned at her and asked her which ones she wanted. We had already made a tentative list.Roma, the Cultural Secretary, made the final selection helped by Sarah."Please give me *Bernadene, Que Sera Sera, Little Serenade, It's Now or Never, Never on a Sunday* and *Cindy oh Cindy*", she told him. Everyone felt that they had made a good choice.

The owner looked gratified at her enthusiasm but the elderly gentleman was plainly disgusted with the whole incident. It was outlandish to see a troop of young girls gallivanting alone without so much as a respectable escort, all of them chattering away like magpies! He said so, adding, "*ki deen kaal poreche, mashai*" (what's the world coming to)! The owner of the shop tried to pacify him, saying that the records the girls had chosen were quite the rage these days. He grunted while we made for the door happily. However, Roma had forgotten an important record. She waved at the salesman, smiled broadly and said,

"Oh and *Remember you're mine*, please." There was an explosion from the elderly gentleman who glared at Roma and said, "Isn't that a rather tall order, Miss, considering you've just met him???"

Love letters with a difference

WHENEVER I think of my college days I inevitably remember our hostel and the larks that formed an integral part of our hostel life.Although we managed to have a jolly time on the whole, there was one rule which caused a great deal of resentment.All our letters were "Censored" by the Assistant Superintendent of our hostel before they were handed over to us in the dining hall at dinner time.

The lady in question also cherished the most unholy suspicion of anything she considered to be a "love letter". It could be a request for contribution from the editor of a student magazine, a graphic description of a cricket match from an old school crony, an invitation to a debate or even an account of an N.C.C. bash.Anything written by a boy who was **not** a brother came under the forbidden category and the lady felt it her duty to pull up the culprit for "encouraging the advances of the opposite sex" in no uncertain terms!And that too in front of the entire hostel crowd who would be present in the dining room at that hour.

Not that this stopped people from having boy-friends!But the boys in question did not dare to write anything except inane nothings which could pass for the harmless rambling of a superannuated grand-uncle. Or else write a pack of postcards instead of an envelope as it was a known fact that the lady barely glanced at the pile of postcards.That is to say, all except Asita's boy-friend, who was "doing his English honours" in Surendranath College.

Asita's boy-friend continued to address big fat envelopes to his inamorata and our superintendent handed them over to her with nothing more than a frown. "Talk of partiality!" cried Rina who had just been severely rebuked because her cousin in Darjeeling had quoted a few lines from Tagore's "Sesher Kavita"!Asita smirked. "His language is just fantastic," she crooned, "Even our Superintendent can't but be impressed by it." The rest of us felt highly annoyed. It seemed extremely unfair, even if it were so!

"Let's have a look at his language," said Reba.

"No fears!" cried Asita, shoving the letter inside her desk and locking it.

But fate played into our hands one day when Asita left her bursting billet-doux on the table by mistake. "Let's now read the fantastic words that have the ability to strike even our honored superintendent dumb!" said Rina and picked up the letter. The rest of us surrounded her joyfully. This is how it began:

"Oh Potentate of my Quintessence,

Although the amalgamation and promulgation of our spirits is tantamount to a paramount phenomenon, you deportment and comportment is beyond my apprehension and comprehension."

"Gosh! What a jaw-breaker!" cried Shikha.

"But what does it mean?" asked Reba.

"And what's comportment?" Subrata asked, looking at me.

"Ask me another," I replied, at a loss for words.

"Well, you're supposed to be doing English Honours too!" said Rina accusingly.

"But we don't go for this sort of vocabulary," I replied meekly.

"No wonder Asita snaffles my dictionary the moment a letter arrives," said Rina.

"Well, at least she is lucky not to have the Superintendent falling over her like a ton of bricks every time she has a letter from him," I said.

"Lucky?" cried my friends together. "You call it LUCK to keep getting stuff that's meant to be a bouquet but sound just like brickbats?"

Remembering a Librarian

What is people's current idea of a librarian? Someone who sits in the library and issues books and keeps the returned ones in their place? Is that all?

During my student days the librarian meant a great deal more. They were knowledgeable people who despite not having read the books knew what they contained and which ones had the best reference material for a chosen subject. Our school had no librarian during my time. There were large book shelves spilling over with books in a hall which all of us – middle school onwards – had access to. Someone, usually one of the nuns, was always there with a huge register to record which books we were returning and which we were taking away to read. She was always ready with suggestions if we told her what we were looking for.It was an informal though workable arrangement.

When I joined college I was greatly impressed by the look of the college library but was told that no one could enter it without a library card. To me the card seemed the key to paradise! However, I was soon disillusioned when I discovered that the first and second year students were not allowed to touch the book shelves or even step in where they were kept. We could merely hand in a request slip with a few choices (we were all allowed to see the catalogue of books) and come back the next day for our books. We were allowed to borrow two books at a time and could change them as often as we liked. Mrs. Savera

Tayyab, our librarian, looked rather stern and we had no occasion to speak to her at that stage.

I realized what a wonderful person and librarian she was only when I was a student of the third year, English Honours. I was just beginning to understand what 'reference work' meant and had no clear idea as to how one selected the right books from an ocean of books! As I searched helplessly among the books I had piled up on my table Savera-di (Perhaps I was the only one to call her that instead of Mrs Tayyab) came and stood beside me.

"Any problem?" she asked.

"I have to write about the favourite themes of the Romantic Poets and I don't know where to find it.

Savera-di walked away without a word but was soon back with three or four volumes and told me, "You'll find it in these books". And I did. I was so thrilled!

I sought her help several times after that and she never failed to find me the right books. I asked her if she was a student of English literature herself. She said, "No. But it is a librarian's job to know about the reference books in the library – what they contain, which of them are important, the latest ones in each subject. He/she has to read reviews, consult the professors if necessary, and order the right books. I take my job very seriously. That is how I am able to help students."I also remember that when I was in my final year Savera-di brought me several rare books belonging to her husband with the stipulation that I must keep and handle them very carefully and return them to her in a week's time. What a wonderfully generous thing to do!

Are there any librarians like Savera-di now? I don't know where she is. But I still remember her fondly and wish there were more like her.

All about "Quotes"

We were in the third year of college at the time. We were reading the poems of Tennyson and our professor had just completed his immortal poem, Ulysses. It had left a good many of us spellbound. All of us - Pass as well as English Honours students - raved about the wonderful lines of the poem, quoting them in and out of season, especially lines like "I will drink life to the lees".

It was a torrid summer and there was no fridge in our hostel (which was Spartan to the extreme although we never gave it a thought). What we missed most was cold water. We managed to buy a large earthen surahi which cooled our drinking water beautifully and we placed it right in the middle of the dormitory so that everyone could share it. The understanding was that we would all take it in turns to keep it filled. But unfortunately the last drinkers often forgot to do it and we found it empty just when someone was dying of thirst. Finally we found that someone had written the following line in chalk on the surahi : "Whoever drinks this surahi to the lees must remember to fill it". It was written by Subrata Sen, a student of Sanskrit Honours. She later became the Principal of Sanskrit College, Calcutta. I wonder where she is and if she remembers the incident.

The Jatra on Viswakarma Puja day

17th of September happens to be my father's birthday and also the day of Viswakarma Puja who is said to be the god of all workers and all who work with gadgets of any kind. Ever since I can remember the two somehow always manage to fall on the same day. Long, ago when I was a child and the cotton mill set up by my grandfather (father's father) was running full swing, the workers of the mill used to celebrate it in a big way. There would be a huge image of Viswakarma followed by *puja, arati*, the cooking of *bhog* (offerings) in enormous vessels, followed by feasting on the same. And it always seemed to me that they were celebrating Baba's birthday as well.

There also used to be a *jatra* at night with a stage put up for the occasion. Jatra in an informal sense meant there were no curtains. One set of players would simply jump down from the stage after the scene and the next set of players would scramble up. This effectively put an end to the hassle of pulling on and off of curtains. As it took place late at night Khukudi (my cousin) and I were considered too young to sit up for the show. Of course my Thakuma (Father's mother) would go along with my mother and aunts, accompanied by my father and uncle to watch it.

One year, however, we were allowed to go because we had begged my kaku (uncle) to plead on our behalf and knew that our grandma would not be able to resist him. However, she made it amply clear that we were to be there for a short while only. Both Khukudi and I were thrilled beyond words because nothing so thrilling had come our way before. We gazed enraptured at the king in gleaming clothes although we could not make out what exactly he was saying. Then the court dancer appeared in a bright red *ghaghra*(flared long skirt) and a golden *chunni* (veil) and started singing. I still remember the lines- *Aakhiyamilaakejiyabharmaakechalenahinjaana* (you looked into my eyes and twisted my heart, now don't go away)

ohohohchalenahinjaana (oh don't go away)

She went round and round the stage as she sang the last line over and over again.

The audience watched avidly for some time but when she repeated *oh ohohohchalenahinjaana*for the twentieth time they grew impatient and someone shouted *aagebadho... aagebadho*(proceed, proceed) . But the dancer paid no heed and went on repeating the line. Finally she came to the centre of the stage, stuck out her tongue and said *Aageyaadnahinhai* (I don't remember any more) and jumped down from the stage, lifting up her long ghaghra and showing fat and hairy legs. It was a man, of course, although Khukudi and I had not realized it before. Grandma felt that we had watched the jatra long enough and packed us off to bed immediately afterwards. So I don't know how it ended.

When We Put up a Play

Thinking of my schooldays inevitably brings to mind the memories of my brief spell as a boarder. Ours was the only English-medium school in the small town that was sleepy and sylvan in those days. There were about a hundred and fifty students in the school out of whom a handful were boarders, both boys and girls. The age of the boys ranged between five and eight. The girls were more in number and though there were some 5-year-olds, quite a few were older. Romola, being the senior- most among us, ruled the roost with a rod of iron. The boys I remember are Kartik, Naresh, Vipin, Vikram and Kamal. The girls were Ruby, Sandra-Margaret, Joan, Chandra, Pushpa and some others. Unfortunately I cannot recall any of their surnames now.I know that Romola is no more or she would have enjoyed remembering the episode. I have no idea where the others are as I never met any of them after I grew up.

To return to my story, we had a "Boarders' Feast" every year. It was a special day when we went for a picnic in the afternoon, had a bang-up supper and ended up with a concert. As a rule Sister Digna who was the Boarders' Mistress was in charge and we had recitations and action songs like "Where are you going to my pretty maid" or "There's a hole in my bucket." This year, however, Romola asked Sister Digna if we might have a play and offered to produce it. Sister Digna must have been quite astounded by such a request but agreed because she always encouraged us to do things on our own.

The rest of us were frankly astonished. "Nothing to gape at," said Romola, "I have thought it all out. We'll have a scene from the Ramayana, the one where Ravan kidnaps Sita.

"But what about the rest of us?" asked Ruby. "A play should include many people, not just two."

"Well, Ram and Laxman can come and cry a little after Sita has been kidnapped. The rest of you can be part of the crowd."

"What crowd?" I asked.

"Don't be so stupid!" said Romola annoyed, "When Ram and Laxman find Sita gone and start crying other people in the forest are bound to come and comfort them."

"But were there other people in the forest?" asked Sandra, "I always thought Ram, Laxman and Sita went for the *banavas* (exile) alone."

"Well, there's got to be some poetic license," said Romola.

"What is poetic license?" asked Chandra who was just five years old.

"It's too bad to be obliged to do a play with a pack of babies!" said Romola in a disgusted voice. "It means, one is allowed to do some things which are not there in the actual story. At least, that's what I think Sister Claudina told us in yesterday's class. You and Pushpa being in the Baby-class (the Nursery was called the Baby-class in those days) would naturally not know anything about it."

"Who will play Ravan, Ram and Laxman?" asked Pushpa curiously.

"Well Vikram is the tallest but unfortunately his face is bandaged because of toothache so he can't be Ravan," said Romoladeciseively. "It had better be Kartik. Naresh and Vipin can be Ram and Laxman. I shall play Sita, of course."

"But Kartik barely comes up to your shoulder," I protested.

"So what? Did Teacher ever say Ravan was very tall?" asked Romola frowning.

"Well, no," I admitted, "I don't remember her saying it."

"There you are! One doesn't have to be tall in order to be a kidnapper", said Romola.

"But Naresh and Vipin are even shorter than Kartik!" I said, "You can't have a husband who barely comes up to your elbow!"

"Ram and Laxman will come into the room only after I have been kidnapped so no one is likely to notice their height," said Romola. "Really, Swapna, you simply must stop making silly comments. Anyone would think that you are jealous because I didn't cast you as Sita."

I shut my mouth after that while Sandra said, "Will you have time to learn all the words? The feast is tomorrow night. And who will write it all down?"

"Nothing to write," said Romola, "We'll make up the words as we go along. Nothing could be simpler!"

"Or you could do that thing – you know, where you have only actions and no words," said Ruby.

"A tableaux!" said Romola, "Yes, that would be a good idea. Come on, folks, let's have the first scene where Ravan dresses up as a beggar and comes to Sita's cottage. I'll sit with a plate of fruits and when I come to give them he can kidnap me."

Romola found a stool and sat holding an empty bowl on her lap. Kartik came to the door but couldn't make out what he should do to call her attention and so started dancing. The dance looked like one from a Hindi film and Romola shook her fist to convey that it was not the right action. But Kartik, totally wrapped up in the dance, went round and round and did not look at her.

"Stop!" cried Sita, "What do you think you are doing?
"

"How else can I make you look at me?" asked Ravan bewildered.

"Stare at me, silly," cried Romola.

"How can I stare at you and dance at the same time?" asked Kartik.

"Who asked you to dance? Tap on the floor and make a noise and I'll look up," said Romola sounding exasperated.

"I think this play is not suitable for a tableaux," I said.

"Very well. Speak up, all of you," said Romola.

The rehearsals proceeded smoothly after that although the argument between Sita and Ravan seemed different every time.

"What are you going to wear?" asked Ruby.

Romola looked stumped. She had not considered this aspect of the matter before. She paused for a moment and said, "I shall drape my scarf over my skirt. The boys can wrap a bath towel around their shorts.

"What if it slips?" asked Naresh.

"Wear a belt over it, stupid!" cried Romola. "Really no one seems to have any common sense these days."

"What about us?" I asked.

"Nothing," said Romola looking annoyed, "The crowd can wear anything and no one will care one way or the other."

Sister Digna looked highly amused when Romola told her about the play which was to be the last item. The programme had the usual round of school songs and recitations. The audience comprised Mother Vera, Sister Bernita, Sister Ethel-reida, Sister Claudina, Sister Hilda, Sister Evelyn and some others plus the white-veiled nuns who saw to the domestic arrangements. And of courseEsthu and Mary who helped Sister Digna look after the boarders, the kitchen team plus all who were not part of the play.

The first scene showed Sita sitting on a stool with a scarf draped all over her. In our hurry we had forgotten to ask for fruits. As there was no place to keep the bowl Romola was obliged to keep it on her lap. Kartik came in draped in a peacock-blue towel and a mustache hurriedly drawn with ink. Everyone roared with laughter. Ravan forgot his lines and cried, "You there, come out at once."

"Ask for the food first, silly," hissed Romola under her breath.

"Gimme those biscuits," stammered Ravan.

"I won't!" said Sita making a face at him.

"I'll.... I'll....pull your hair if you don't," said Ravan, holding on to his towel with one hand and tugging at Sita's plaits with the other.

As this was clearly not a part of the plan Sita gave him a resounding slap. Ravan stumbled against the stool and fell down with a crash, bursting into a loud volley of howls.

"Stupid cry-baby!" said Sita in a disgusted voice.

"Kartik bhaiya!" cried Laxman and burst into tears. Ram quietly picked up the bowl of biscuits and made short work of the lot.

The audience was in hysterics by now, even Mother Vera was mopping her eyes.

Sita stood up majestically and pushed the sobbing Ram and Ravan out of the stage and said, "Catch me doing a play again with cry-babies like you!"

And thus ended our play, while the audience clapped enthusiastically amidst loud guffaws.

"It was such a tragic play and we wanted to have you all in tears!" said Romola.

"Well, you succeeded admirably!" said Sister Hilda laughing.

Needh-wa

I remember, some years back there was a TV programme where the popular comedian Raju Shrivastava demonstrated how a person from Bihar would recite the well known nursery rhyme, "Jack and Jill went up the hill".

The first line was:
Jack-wa aur Jill-wa
Upargaye hill-wa
paniabharankevaste

It made me remember an incident in school. When I first joined school we had to learn just two languages, English and our mother tongue which was Bengali in my case. Hindi was made a compulsory subject only when I was in Class 8. All of us with different mother tongues had simple textbooks, quite different from those who had Hindi as their mother tongue. There used to be a joint grammar class of classes 8,9 and 10. During one such class the teacher was teaching us synonyms and mentioned "needh" as a synonym for "ghosla" (nest).

My friend Maitry who was in class 9 asked, "Do you really have the term "needh" in Hindi, Teacher?" "Why not?" asked our teacher in some surprise. Maitry said, "I thought it would be needh-wa" with a perfectly straight face.

The rest of the class was in splits of laughter. Fortunately it was the last class and the bell rang just then or else.....!!

The Tutor Trap

It happened when my grandfather took my sister and me for a brief visit to Patna to see to some repairs in his house there. We didn't know the current occupants of the house next door but I remembered that it belonged to friend of grandfather's. Our first floor bedroom was directly opposite theirs. We were somewhat stunned to see half a dozen boys, aged between 7 and 12, clamouring all over the bed, the dressing table and the chest of drawers, making more noise than a dozen boys put together! A young man tried to maintain some sort of order but failed miserably. We couldn't help wondering who they were and asked our caretaker.

"Oh just some woman distantly related to the owner whose husband is posted outside Patna. She lives here alone with the boys."

Next morning grandfather told us to ask the lady if she could spare the gardener for a moment as he wanted some information. The pandemonium had already started in the upstairs room and the lady, obviously the mother of the boys, sat chewing a half-ripe guava in the front room.She frowned when we told her what we wanted and sent for the gardener.

"Are those your sons in the room upstairs?" I asked.

"Yes, five of them. And their tutor. My eldest lives with his grandparents."

"Don't they go to school?" asked my sister surprised.

"No. I calculated the cost of school fees for five and realized that it would be far cheaper to engage a tutor."

We were too stunned to reply. Although unmarried (at the time), I was sure that most parents thought differently! I also remembered that there was a study downstairs used by the elder son of the houseand was shared by his younger brother, our one-time playmate.

"Isn't there a study downstairs?" I asked.

"Yes, but the bedroom upstairs is the only room in the house with an attached toilet," replied the lady.

"Does that matter?" asked my sister bewildered.

"Of course it matters!" growled the lady, "I can't let that crowd loose and have them turn the entire house topsy- turvy! Now they know there is simply no excuse to step outside the room. I have also kept a huge ghada (pot) of water inside. I had used clay ones at first but after they broke three in a row I replaced it with a brass one."

"Oh," said my sister, "And what about their meals?"

"I let them come down for half an hour in the afternoon for lunch keeping a strict eye on them and their tutor.And escort them back the moment they finish their food. I send up a cup of tea and glasses of milk for the boys at 4.30.The tutor leaves at 5 PM. I wanted him to stay until 6 but he refused point blank. Said he couldn't possibly stay for more than 8 hours.

I suddenly remembered that it was nearly 8 PM when we reached Patna last night and the pandemonium was very much on.

"But we saw him around 8 last night," said my sister.

"Oh that's because I had been to the cinema and found there were no tickets. So I had to wait for the next show. The key was with me, of course." said the lady.

"Key?" we asked bewildered.

"I always lock them and the tutor in the room as soon as he arrives," she remarked, "Why do you look surprised? Surely you don't imagine that I'd risk any of them running about the place the moment my back is turned?"

A College for women

I wonder if anyone who is familiar with the flourishing K.B. Women's College of today remembers what it was like when it first started. There were seven of us plus our principal. We had no college building, no campus and no set up of any kind! Besides, most of us were fresh from the university and without any experience. Including our principal, whom we called Bari didi.

The entire town was wary of the newly founded college and we might have sunk without a trace the very first month but for a few staunch supporters. The most important was Sri Krishan Ballav Sahay, a minister, who strongly felt that there should be a college for girls in the town, however small, and gifted us a fairly big piece of land where the college was built later. The other was Rani Chatterjee, the principal of the Govt. Girls' school who felt the same and very kindly let us hold classes in a shed behind the main school building.

The shed, divided into small cubicles, had been built for storing extra and useless things. The rooms were in a single line, tiny and without windows where nothing more than a small desk and a few chairs could fit. But we were perfectly happy despite the Spartan surroundings. In any case, we took most of the classes either in the lawn or some other part of the school garden. Our handful students belonged to two categories – those who had done so badly in their Higher Secondary exams that they simply didn't dare to seek admission in the famous and well established St. Columba's College which had recently become a co-ed one. The second category comprised those whose fathers were so much against their daughters studying with boys that they reluctantly agreed to let them come to us. Luckily the girls were happy to have a brood of young lecturers and seemed to enjoy our classes and took down copious notes which made us happy.When one is young everything appears rosy and we took everything as a huge joke and laughed and chattered the time away taking our classes to the best of our ability and spending the free periods discussing books, films and other trivia.

Before long our college became the main topic for discussion, even among my grandpa's contemporaries.

"What's the use of opening a shop if there are no buyers?" asked a crony of my grandfather's.

"I understand there are more teachers than students there," stated another.

"I feel sorry for the *master-ni* s," said a third.

"They'll shut down within a month, you'll see!" remarked the last one somewhat gleefully.

"No need to be so pessimistic," replied my grandfather, "They are just starting. The college will soon grow."

Although we were livid at first at being referred to as "*mastar-ni*" by most people we were finally compelled to accept their mode of address. To most of the locals, the entire teaching community had just two names – *master* and *mastar-ni* – no matter **where** they taught, school, college or university.

Only the Pre-university class was an exception which had a decent number of girls. Mrs. Chatterjee, the principal of the Govt. Girls' School, had actually bullied some fathers into letting them remain in our college by refusing to give them their transfer certificates. She was a formidable figure and thought bullying for a good cause perfectly fair. She asked the fathers frankly why they were so keen to send their girls to a co-ed college. Strangely enough, no one said, "Because it is a good and well established college with experienced staff". Instead, they offered all kinds of strange reasons, one of them being, *"meri beti bahut sharmileehai. Ladkonkesaathpadegi to smart ban jayegi"*(my daughter is very shy. Studying with boys will make her smart.). Mrs. Chatterjee scoffed and replied, "She can very well afford to wait another year and complete her Pre-University here. She can join St. Columba's for her B.A. and become as smart as you please."

As far as we could see, the students didn't seem at all upset to continue in their old school campus and were quite pleased to have a pack of young and inexperienced staff, not half as strict as their teachers in school had been. Nevertheless, Bari didi and Mrs. Chatterjee called an urgent meeting to discuss how we could possibly get more students.

"Perhaps we should organize some sort of campaign and visit people personally," suggested Bari didi.

"We have to convince them that it is important for women to be educated," said Mrs. Chatterjee.

I remembered my mother who had been married off as soon as she completed her matriculation and her tough struggle to study further, battling through hundreds of obstacles to reach the Ph. D level eventually. Perhaps there were other women who had also dreamt of going to college once but couldn't because of circumstances. Gradually our cause became broader – not just getting more students but also convincing stay-at-home women to go for higher study. Mrs. Chatterjee knew most of the people in our small town and suggested families where we were likely to find future students.Bari didi was the leader of the expedition and we accompanied her, turn by turn.

It was a never- to- be- forgotten experience! There were some who did not let us meet the womenfolk at all and told us straight out that they were not interested in letting ANY of them go to college, young or old. A woman's true place, they told us, was AT HOME! They were dead against their gallivanting outside its walls. Some heard Bari didi politely and offered us tea but told us firmly that they were not in favour of higher studies for women as it was a waste of time and money. Bari didi was upset by their attitude. "They seem to be living in the 19th century!" she told us regretfully, "Should we call it a day?"

"Never!" we cried together, "We shall try a different locality tomorrow."

Our determination paid off. Bari didi having realized that the people who had the final say would not agree to spend money on what they felt to be a useless cause. So she took care to announce that these students – especially any elderly ones who cared to join – would not have to pay college fees. We could feel a visible thaw in the icy atmosphere after that. The men folk realized that ours was not a clever ploy for making money and were willing to listen to Bari didi's words. Some of them relented. As a result we managed to acquire some more students. A few of them were seniors who had been married off soon after their matriculation years ago and now had grown up children. But they had once cherished the desire to go to college in their hearts and were elated to get an unexpected opportunity. "But we have forgotten all that we had once learned," said more than one lady, "Can we possibly do it?" "Of course you can," said Bari didi, "One can study at any age, if one really wants to."

The next day Bari didi had an urgent meeting with us. She warned us to be very careful, especially with the senior students, as they were likely to be rather touchy/nervous for daring to do such an unconventional thing. Apart from a few single ladies there were two mother-daughter teams and one saas-bahu team. Both ladies from the mother-daughter team were eager and looked really happy to be back to learning once again. They listened carefully, took down notes and sometimes asked questions.

But one of the married ladies looked at me somewhat contemptuously, wondering if I were stating facts or pulling a fast one. She did not remain quiet much longer. One day suddenly in the middle of a lecture she burst out, "*Lekin Bandana ka baapboltahai ki aisanahinhai*" (Bandana's father says what you are saying is not correct). Apparently Bandana was her daughter. I turned a lurid purple at the unexpected assault. Then I asked, "*to kaisahaibataiye*" (then tell me the correct answer). She gave me a broad smile and said, "*wo to maalumnahin, lekin Bandana ka baapboltahai hi aapkoshayadiskebaarepooramaalumnahin. Bahut kothinbishaybastuhaina*" (I don't know that, but Bandana's father says, possibly you do not know all the facts. After all, it is a tough subject). She continued to quote "Bandana ka baap" in and out of season and I had to learn to shrug off her comments.

Although the *bahu* (daughter-in-law) was a bright student the *saas*(mum-in-law) in the saas-bahu team who made it a point to dress up within an inch of her life looked bored most of the time and kept whispering to anyone who sat next to her. She had to be pulled up tactfully as she disturbed those who wanted to attend. It happened in everyone's class, including Bari didi's who finally ventured to ask her if she enjoyed her classes. "Of course I don't," she answered at once, "I don't care about studies." "We were taken aback. "Then why did you join?" asked Bari didi looking surprised. "Only because I wanted to keep an eye on my bahu", she answered. Poor Bari didi did not know what to make of it! Nor did the rest of us! "But this is a girls' college," said Bari didi at last, "Why do you need to keep an eye on her?" The saas stood up majestically and said, "*aajkal ki chokriyon ka kuchbharosanahin! Nazar to rakhna hi partahai*!" (one can't trust the girls of today. It is necessary to keep an eye on them).

When I remember the incident I feel sorry that Jeetendra was a young hero of Bollywood at the time and Ekta Kapoor was not even born. Or else she mighthave picked up a few novel ideas for her saas-bahu serials!

The Notice Board

Although our college had a big and prominent notice board right in front of the Principal's office it remained blank and empty most of the time. For one thing, there being such few students we preferred to make our announcements personally in class. In any case, we seldom had anything important enough to put up there during mid-session. Sometimes when my students did badly in a college test I threatened to put up their marks on the notice board for everyone to see. But the girls knew that I was not serious so they merely grinned.

One morning as I walked into my class I remembered that I had meant to give a test to the final year students. I had a severe toothache and was feeling mad with the entire world. My students told me that they were not prepared and begged me to postpone it to the next week. I might have done it readily enough under normal circumstances.But this morning the entire class seemed to be in a flutter, giggling, nudging each other and staring at the door. Even Sulochana, who was a model of propriety on other days, seemed restless and jittery. No, I told myself, I just have to be firm with them or else they'd get totally out of hand.

I wrote the questions on the black-board and asked them to get on. They pretended to write but continued to stare at the door periodically. When the bell rang for recess I remained glued to my seat going through their papers. What the others had managed to scribble was bad enough but Sulochana's lines barely made sense. What on earth was wrong with the girl?

"This is outrageous!" I said, slashing an entire paragraph with red pencil. "I shall really put up your marks on the notice board. This is beyond a joke!"

"Oh please don't Ma'am," cried the entire class in panic while Sulochana dissolved into a flood of tears. "Then you shouldn't have handed in such rubbish!" I said, marching to the notice board and pinning up the marks. Sulochana who usually topped the class had the lowest marks of all.

Just then a couple of ladies alighted from a car outside the gate and made for the Principal's office. One of the ladies paused midway and walked up to the notice board seeing the crowd in front. She whisked out her glasses from her bag, put them on and stared at the notice board. Then she looked carefully at the list I had just put up and muttered, "Disgraceful! Obviously her parents were lying!" Needless to say, I had no idea what she was talking about.

When I came back to the classroom everyone looked at me reproachfully.

"How could you do this to her?" said one of my students. "We thought you were our well-wisher!" Sulochana continued to sob.

"What are you talking about?" I asked intrigued, "What have I done? It's you who have disgraced me by doing so badly in the test."

"That was Sulochana's prospective mother-in-law who came to see her unofficially," said another of my students. "And now you have ruined her chances by putting up her marks on the notice board!"

"Good gracious! Why on earth didn't you tell me earlier?" I asked. But the die had been cast.

"You never gave us a chance!" they said in a chorus.

"But what about her exams?" I asked. "Sulochana will be sitting for her BA finals next month."

"These people don't care about degrees!" said one of my students.

"Well, I do," I said, "And I always thought Sulochana was serious about her studies."

"I am," sobbed Sulochana, "And I want to sit for my exams."

"Then why all this weeping and wailing because the match is likely to be broken?" I asked.

"I didn't want the whole college to know that I've been rejected," said Sulochana wiping her eyes, "And now they do! It's such a disgrace."

But disgrace or not, that match was broken and Sulochana graduated with excellent marks and got married to a really nice boy.

Post Script

Three years passed in the blink of an eye. We were really excited when all our girls managed to clear the Pre-University exam and came back to do their BA. The town that had been eyeing us all this time with suspicion and disapproval admitted that we were not as useless as they had feared despite being green in experience. Mrs. Chatterjee and Bari didi felt we had done a good job. Our new college building was coming up and its future seemed secure.

My idyllic existence as a lecturer came to an end when the day of my wedding was finalized and I had to leave for Calcutta. I announced it just a day before leaving and everyone, especially Bari didi, was really annoyed because there was no time to arrange a proper farewell for me. The students somehow got to know about it and landed up with a garland and a lovely bouquet. Bari didi asked them to put a table and the chairs outside while she sent for hot *samosas* and *gulab jamuns* for everyone. Though totally informal, it was a cordial and jovial party which all of us enjoyed. But Bari Didi was really upset because she had meant to read out a proper "Address" for the occasion.

We were just about to disperse when Maulavisa'ab suddenly stood up and announced that he wanted to say a few words. Everyone was astonished, to say the least! MaulaviSa'ab, the only senior and elderly person in the staff, came to take the Urdu classes. He came in quietly, and sat in a corner reading whenever he was not taking classes. People hardly noticed him because he spoke to no one and never looked up from his books.

He took out a scrap of paper on which he had been scribbling during the impromptu party and read out a *sher*(couplet) -

Kaun is bagh se bagh-e-sabajaatihai

Dil ko khamosh aur maghmoomkiyejaatihai

*(*A flower departs from this garden

Making all hearts still and sad*)*

Then he handed me the scrap of paper and vanished before I could thank him. For a while everyone was too stunned to speak. Finally Bari didi said, "Well, Miss Sen, I am glad someone spoke!" The lines were written in Urdu which I could not read. But I am surprised that I still remember the lines even after all these years. Perhaps because no one ever wrote a sher for me either before or after!

Learning To Be A Housewife

Drumsticks with a Difference

WHEN my husband had the first posting of his career in a small town of Bihar he grumbled, not because he did not like the place, but because his knowledge of Hindi was very poor.In spite of assuring me—and everyone else—that he had passed the Hindi test at the Academy of Administration with just a little short of flying colours, he understood very little of the language and was far worse when it came to speaking it.

However, the clerks and inspectors in his office spoke English after a fashion.So he did not have too bad a time.But he grew totally tongue-tied when it came to dealing with the orderlies and left them severely alone as a rule.

In a few months' time he acquired more confidence and lost his terror of Hindi.In fact, he soon assured me that there was nothing to it, after all.Except for changing the suffixes of certain words.

"Changing the suffixes?" I asked amazed. "Well, yes," he said with the air of a research scholar. "Most words in Hindi have an 'aa' sound.What is 'jeere' in

Bengali is 'jeera' in Hindi, 'heere' is 'heera', "cheede" is 'chuda' and so on."

Before I could point out that such over-simplification could lead to troublehe said, "Most Hindi words are the same as the Bengali ones, anyway.It's merely a question of pronouncing them with a Hindi accent."

This theory not only cured his tongue-tied state but also led to his using Bengali words—with a Hindi accent—with such wild abandon that his staff grew doubtful about their own knowledge of the Hindi vocabulary.

Feeling well pleased with life, my husband asked me one morning if I knew how to cook drumsticks. "Of course", I replied, with the rash confidence of one whose culinary experience was barely two months old.

I'll get Ramjatan to fetch some," he said. Ramjatan was his orderly. A nice old man who sometimes dropped in at our place to lend me a hand here and there.Time was when my husband would have sent Ramjatan to me to do any explaining that he needed.But he did not think it necessary any longer.

I waited for the drumsticks all morning.But there was no trace of Ramjatan.When he eventually turned up, empty handed, he looked troubled, confused and annoyed.

"What is the matter?" I asked him curiously, He ignored my question. "Have you quarreled with Saab?" he asked me without any preamble. "Make it up with him immediately or you entire life will be ruined."

"But what is wrong?" I asked, astounded, "What has he told you?"

He asked me to get some . . . some. . . oh, I can't say it!" and he covered his face with his hands.

"Come on," I said puzzled, "What on earth did he ask for?"

"He said. . . he said … get me some sajna from the bazaar"!

I could not help laughing.So this was what his "Suffix-changing" had led to!Turning the Bengali "Sajne"(drumstick) into "Sajna"

sweetheart/beloved).

Ramjatan gave me a reproachful look and said: "I told him that I could not and that he should not have asked for such a thing. But he only shouted and said, "Get me the sajna and never mind its quality."

A Fishy Tale

It happened during my husband's posting in a small town. We were just married and setting up our first home.We lived on the outskirts of the main city, far away from the congested area, in a part that could almost be called sylvan.It suited us fine in every respect except for one thing.There was hardly any market to speak of.Nothing but a few villagers sitting by the roadside with a handful of vegetables.The vegetables were fresh and cheap but sadly lacking in variety.All said and done, one couldn't live on lauki(gourd), tori (ridge gourd) and sitaphal (pumpkin) day in and day out!A man sometimes turned up at the gate with fresh chicken but there was no fish to be had. We had no idea where the fish-market was located or if there was one.Our neighbours, being strict vegetarians, had no idea either.

Then one afternoon I was rudely awakened from my siesta by a determined hammering on my door.I opened it to find a man clutching a huge "Katla" fish in his arms. "You eat fish, don't you?" he asked without any preamble. "Take it.Eight rupees a kilo," I was delighted – though somewhat taken aback by his abrupt manners. "You will have to cut it," I told him. "No time," he grunted, "I'll just weigh it."

"I can't possibly take it unless you cut it," I said firmly.He muttered under his breath, "Get me a knife or a chopper – FAST!I can't wait!" He cut the fish anyhow, literally snatched the money from my hand and made off with limping steps.I couldn't help wondering why he was in such a tearing hurry!

He turned up again a few days later with a "Rahu" fish.What's more, He brought his own chopper this time.I heaved a sigh of relief."Fifteen rupees," he said, weighing the fish. I handed him two tenners.

"Give me the exact amount," he growled, "I haven't any change on me." "Nor have I," I said, "Wait until I get it from my landlady."

"No, no," he shouted, "I'm in a hurry. I can't wait that long. Take it for ten."

Once again he limped off with what seemed incredible speed. He came quite regularly and every time it was the same story! Every time he seemed to be in a desperate hurry to leave. I took him for a harmless nut.

Some months later we made the acquaintance of a local gentleman who invited us to see his farmhouse. "I suppose, being Bengalis, you love fish?" he said with a loud guffaw. "I only wish I could give you some!I do have a huge tank in my farm that is teeming with fish. But I'm driven plain crazy by a rascally sneak-thief who steals my fish regularly and sells it off to the first customer he comes across.Fellow with a limp.I haven't been able to catch him yet. But I'm determined to do it!" He laughed ruefully and added "I don't see why I should bore you about our local thieves. Being new to place, you wouldn't know a thing about them – would you?"

The Bull that refused to Budge

MY husband has always been interested in gardening.So when he was posted ina small, picturesque town and discovered two empty fields attached to his new office-cum residence, he was ecstatic. "I'll have a real garden for you," he said enthusiastically, "Just wait for a few months"

Frankly speaking, I hadn't much faith in his dream-garden.To start with, he had no experience in the matter, Secondly, who knew what the soil was like.Thirdly, one could hardly expect one's very first attempt to be a success!But there was something special about the place after all!Incredible as it might seem, the seeds really took to the soil and the upcoming seedlings made a lush green carpet all around that was very pleasing to the eye.Before long the cabbages and the cauliflowers, the tomatoes, beans and peas came up in a riot."How lovely it will be to have curries made from vegetables that we have grown ourselves," said my husband. I agreed, little knowing what fate had in store for us!

A few days later we woke up to find an enormous bull standing right in the middle of the garden, devouring the peas.There was no trace of the cauliflower plants. And it looked as if the tomatoes had never existed!The cabbages and the rest of the plants lay scattered, limp and trampled upon.

My husband was in a royal rage, "Who let in that bull?" he cried wrathfully.No one knew!The fencing was intact and the gates shut.Yet the bull stood blinking at us as if it were a part of the garden. "Lock it up in the courtyard," said my husband to the orderly. "I'm going to fine whoever it belongs to.

Ruining my garden like this!" The bull was locked up in the courtyard.It roamed about, making short work of every shrub and plant therein.A whole day passed without anyone claiming it. "Well," said my husband, "Ask the owner to take it away. I'll excuse the fine this time."

Another day passed.The orderly complained that the bull had attacked the line of washing and had chewed bits from all the clothes, thereby ruining them.The cook was hysterical because her sari had been a new one and I was compelled to give her one of mine.Another day passed.

"Drive out the bull," ordered my husband."Let the owner hunt for it!"

But it turned out to be a hopeless task!The bull refused to be driven out and ran around in circles when chased. "Can't anyone drive it out?" asked my husband exasperated. Apparently no one could. He totally refused to leave the courtyard.

The bull also nibbled bits of the mat belonging to the gardener, the ropes of his cot and the old sacks in the shed. "Can't you really take is away?" I implored, looking at the gardener. "I'll give you a fiver, if you do."

"No. You can see that I can't!" grunted the gardener.

"A tenner, then," I said. In those days that's how we referred to ten-rupee and five-rupee notes.

The gardener agreed with the air of doing me a favour and drove it out with what seemed incredible ease.My husband shook his head and said, "So it's you who ended up paying the fine, eh?" I laughed ruefully!What else could one do with a bull that refused to budge?

Let in a Vet

THE VET standing at our doorstep, bag in hand, gave me his usual toothless grin and said, "Fetch me a pan of boiling water, will you?"

"But my husband is on tour," I mumbled. "I had asked you to come next week, didn't I?"

"I don't see how it matters," he said striding into the room and dumping his bag on the table, "The shot isn't for your husband.It is for the dog."

"I mean there isn't anyone to help you," I said, "I can't hold him.He is too big and strong for me."

The vet peered over his glasses. "Are you talking of your dog?" he asked. "Naturally," I said indignantly.

"I never said I needed your help, did I?" he said, getting out his syringe and needle," I am perfectly capable of handling him or any other beast, for that matter.Single handed!" I recalled the previous occasion when he had come to give Rocky his six-monthly shot. "My husband had to hold Rocky jolly hard the last time you were here" I said, "I can't do it."

"Believe me, Madam, it was totally unnecessary," he told me. "Your husband held him because he wanted to and not because I told him to.Just bring him here and leave it all to me."

"I told you he's out on tour," I said frowning.

"I was talking of your dog," he said.

"Very well," I said and called Rocky.

Rocky dashed in growling.Probably he still remembered his last shot.The vet jumped up."Good gracious, where is his leash?Tie him to that window.Yes, that's right." Then he threw me a piece of string. "Now tie his mouth like this.Yes, that's the way.No, no, not so loose.It will come undone the moment he tries to bark.One knot, then another.Yes, that's about right.Could have been a little tighter, though.Never mind.Now go and fetch that water while I get the shot ready.And see that the dog doesn't free his mouth."

"I thought you were going to handle him all by yourself." I said sarcastically. But it seemed to go over his head.

He glared at me. "The day I need assistance handling animals I'll give up being a vet." He said firmly. "Now come and sit near the dog.Good God, what's the point of your sitting on the chair?Sit on the floor next to him.That's right.Now put his head against your shoulder.Like this.Just so that he can't move.Now clasp him tightly with both hands.Gracious, are your hands made of butter or what?Clasp him tight.No, no, tighter.See that he isn't able to wriggle or move an inch."

I held on, nearly strangling Rocky in my attempt to hold him tight.But he jumped up in spite of it.The vet started.The ampoule slipped from his hand and crashed on the floor.

I heaved a sigh of relief. "I suppose it happened because you like doing things single-handed?" I said.He grunted, collected his bag and stomped out of the room.

Changing Attitudes

I was visiting my Grand-uncle in Delhi soon after my marriage. My Grand-uncle, who had been an extremely popular teacher at the Calcutta University, always had droves of students (from India and abroad) visiting him at all hours to pay their respects. Normally I kept out of the way. But one day he sent for me when one of his ex-students was visiting him and asked me if I remembered him as we were both from the Calcutta University and had graduated the same year.

In those days it was usual to know students from other colleges as there were not too many who went in for their Masters.I glanced at him and recognized him instantly. He was one of those haughty and snooty guys with his nose perpetually in the air. Also, he was one of those insufferable ones who imagined that every female was falling in love with him! Grand-uncle, a bachelor and always fathoms deep in academics, asked him if he knew me. He replied condescendingly, "Oh well, the Darbhanga and Asutosh Buildings (the two main buildings in our University Campus) are teeming with girls all the time. Rather difficult to recall them individually."

"Of course," said Grand-uncle. "I expect it's difficult."

"Besides, there were too many fellows from the Science Campus who made a beeline for our Arts Campus all the time," I said, giving him a glaring look. "We only thought of them as a pack and not persons," I said.

Grand-uncle introduced us meekly and both of us nodded coldly and sat in grim silence.

"You know, B. (the student) has just been posted in Dehradoon," said Grand-uncle, "He has been telling me how nice the place is. S. (me), by the way, lives in Gaya where her husband has just been posted."

B. gave me a pitying look and burst forth into a description of snow ranges and roses in the hills of Mussoori. Unfortunately there was nothing flattering I could say about Gaya so I spoke of the peace and tranquillity of Bodh-Gaya and the tourists who visit the place from far off lands to see the beautiful Buddhist shrines.

"Oh Bodh-Gaya isn't Gaya, you know," he said in a sneering voice.

"Well, Mussoori isn't Dehradoon either!" I said triumphantly.

What followed was an uncomfortable silence with Grand-uncle looking at us curiously. Fortunately it was rather late and B. decided to take his leave.

As chance would have it, I met B. again, this time also at my Grand-uncle's place, nearly three years later. My first daughter was just a few months old at the time. B., I was told, was also married with a little girl. But this time the moment B. heard that I was there he dashed into the room where I was trying to put my baby to sleep, peeped at her and asked, "Are you giving her Farex (a baby food) already?"

"No, my doctor wanted me to give her Nestum (another baby food)," I replied mildly.

"Does she wake up and cry at night? What do you do then?" he asked me, pulling up a chair and sitting down.

One eager question followed another as I answered them to the best of my ability with the authority of a mother whose baby was a month older than his. I asked him questions about his baby too. After what seemed a very short time Grand-uncle came into the room and looked at us in round-eyed astonishment. "I was under the impression that you both didn't ... err... approve of one another?" he remarked, "But you've been chatting nineteen to the dozen for nearly an hour!"

"Have we?" I asked, looking sheepish.

"That long?" asked B. looking amazed.

Being parents had changed both our worlds and all the baby-chatter had changed our outlook too. The babies were the centre of our world now – not ourselves!

The Follies of Freelancing

NOT all husbands take kindly to their wives taking up a career.Specially one as erratic as "freelancing" which neither has the lure of a regular silver-tonic nor the importance of a snooty designation.Moreover, wrestling with one's Muse inevitably leads to spasms of forgetfulness, resulting in burnt milk, unsalted curries and empty lunch-boxes.But after a while the family usually learns to shrug off such omissions as something to be put up with. Unfortunately it was otherwise with my neighbours!Things were fine so long as I was known as just a housewife of a rather non-descript brand.But the moment the children started babbling about "Mummy's stories," the fat was in the fire.

"I hear you write?" asked Mrs. V, my next-door neighbor, accusingly. I nodded, wondering what was coming next.

"Scandalous," said Mrs. V shaking her knitting-needles, "People write more rubbish these days than is good for anybody! A married woman has no right to indulge in such tomfoolery."

"But I started writing long before I was married," I protested.

"A woman who prefers the pen to the knitting-needle is abnormal," said Mrs. V.

I kept quiet.

"For which paper do you write, anyway?" she asked, "And I suppose you are related to the editor?" I hastened to deny it. "Don't tell me," she said, "Nothing gets published unless you are related to the editor. My daughter-in-law once sent a story but it was sent back because the editor did not know her personally."

"Why didn't she send it elsewhere?" I asked meekly. "They are all the same," said Mrs. V with a snort, "My daughter writes beautiful poems. But the editor keeps rejecting them for the same reason." "Did he say so?" I ventured to ask. "Is there any need to say what is obvious?" she asked angrily. There was a grim silence while I tried to think of something to say.

"Why don't you start writing too?" I suggested, "I'm sure you can."

"Of course I can!" said Mrs. V impatiently, "Any fool can write! But what will happen to my knitting if I waste my time writing?"

What indeed!I thought of timid Mr. V in his pullovers of shocking-pink, peacock-blue, poison-green and post-office-red, looking the picture of misery because grey happened to be his favouritecolour. Mrs. V gave me a scathing look. "I prefer womanly accomplishments," she said, "I feel so sorry for Mr. Dutta who has nothing but a grey and a cream pullover and has to take turns wearing them.Unfortunately a man has to pay for his wife's folly!"

She picked up her knitting, (a lurid purple with orange blobs) and ambled out majestically.

Not too elevating!

I HAVE always been allergic to lifts.The more sophisticated they are, the less I like them.They give me the eerie sensation of sinking down a well or being hauled up by a crane. When visiting buildings with lifts I always took for the staircase with a nonchalant air, turning a blind eye to the wide eyed stares that invariably follow me.If I come across an acquaintance, I pretend it is for the sake of my figure.

But I was compelled to revise my policy when I dropped in at one of Delhi's umpteen "Bhawans" and realized that my husband's office was on the eleventh floor. I had been shopping in Janpath and was dead tired and thought it would be nice to pay him a surprise visit and wangle a cup of tea at the same time.

"A lady to see you, sir," the man at the reception informed him over the phone. I asked if I might put in a word.He nodded.

"Could you come down for a sec?" I suggested. "What for?" he asked sounding surprised, "Why don't you come up?"

"Well it is your lift.It makes me jittery."

"For goodness' sake, keep your voice low," he hissed."Folks around here will think that you've come from a village."

He strode into the reception hall after a few minutes, trying not to look annoyed. "Come on," he said, walking towards the only lift that appeared to be working.I followed meekly."Can't think how any educated person can be afraid of a lift," he muttered.

"I always think it is going to crash!" I replied sheepishly.

"Well it did this morning." He admitted. "Only three floors, though.We were too tightly packed to be really hurt."

"What did you do?" I asked.

"Climb out, of course," he said matter-of-factly."It's silly to be afraid of lifts.Haven't you seen the alarm bell?"

"It would be of no use if the electricity fails," I said.

"Oh well, lifts are perpetually being repaired.Someone would be sure to find you sooner or later."

"What if a sudden holiday is declared just then?" I argued. "A V.I.P might choose to kick the bucket when I'm trapped inside one.Then they'll find my skeleton."

"Hardly," he scoffed. "At the most, they might find a corpse."

When it was time to leave I used the stairs in spite of his protests.Just as I reached the ground-floor landing, there came an ominous clang. It's one of those lifts again," said someone in the queue.

I thanked my stars and braced myself for a climb to the 11th floor.I had left my house-keys on his table!

When you go by Ads….!

I HAVE a tremendous weakness for kitchen gadgets.Probably because I hate housework!So any machine which is supposed to lessen it in any way has me all agog.What's more, I have the fatal tendency to swallow ads wholesale minus the proverbial pinch of salt!Well, that's what prompted me to go in for my new mixie. I am talking of the time when they were very new in the market and were of the most basic kind.

"Will it really save either time or labour?" asked by husband skeptically as I staggered in with the enormous bundle. Mixies were rather large and cumbersome in those days.

"Of course it will," I said indignantly. "It is supposed to do just about everything!"

I tried kneading first. The machine which was supposed to operate sans noise or vibrations played a dizzy jig on the table, making it rattle in an intoxicated manner.

"I thought the blasted thing was supposed to be noiseless," bellowed my husband, looking up from his newspaper, "This makes more noise than all your previous ones put together!"

"Possibly a new mixie is like a new shoe," I said, "It's bound to creak at first," I said hopefully.

"At least I hope you can make cookies now," said my younger daughter. "You couldn't with your previous mixie!"

"Of course I shall be able to make them!" I said.

But I had spoken too soon. It is true that my previous mixi was not suitable for tough kneading but my new one had no intention of doing it either! I put in the flour, the butter and the sugar-and the whole mixture went round and round without so much as forming a ball! It would do nothing more until I put in a bit of liquid and by then it was too soft and no use as cookie-dough.

"Mummy, could you possible put away all these bits and pieces somewhere?" said my elder daughter. "I have to submit a design tomorrow and this is the only big table in the house." I looked frantically for a container which could house all these queer-shaped discs and blades but could not.

"Don't tell me you forgot to ask for the container? The ad said they were giving a free container for keeping the parts," said my younger daughter.

"Well no," I said sheepishly. "The salesman said they were just for the first few customers. The last one was given away three months ago."

I hastily shoved the parts to a corner of the table.

I next tried slicing and shredding the vegetables. After all it was the cutting of vegetables which had always been my bugbear and the main reason for my going in for the new mixie. However, the slices and shreds were paper-thin and turned into a multi-coloured jumble even before they were parboiled!

"Why on earth couldn't you dice the vegetables instead of making a lump like that?" enquired my husband.

"You can't dice things in a kitchen machine," I said.

"Well, shred them thicker in that case."

"You can't adjust the thickness either! Or chop them any other way," I said.

"Then why on earth do they lie in all those ads?" cried my younger daughter indignantly.

"I suppose because they have to sell the things somehow," I replied, feeling angrier by the minute for being taken in by a mere ad!

"I told you so!" said all three together and for once, I took it lying down!

"It's all very well to sneer," I said finally. "But what am I to do?"

"No problem," said my husband with a chuckle. "We've a show-case, don't we?"

Beaten at the Post

MRS V. waved a long envelop under my nose and said, "Where is your husband?I want him to post this letter personally and see that it reaches."

"But, but he isn't in the Postal department anymore," I stammered.

Mrs V's eyes flashed an I-told-you-so look as she said, "Not there anymore?Ah, gave the wrong change once too often, did he?"

"Well, not quite," I said, smothering a laugh. "He has gone on deputation.To the Ministry of Finance."

Mrs V glared at me accusingly. "What for?" she cried. "Since he wasn't handling cash earlier, of what earthly use would he be at the Ministry of Finance?" Are they opening a new post office there?I suppose their letters are going astray like mine and they think it would be useful to have a postal man around, one familiar with all the beats."

I explained patiently that he had **not** gone as a postal man.Besides, only the postmen were familiar with the beats, not the officers. Mrs. V frowned and asked, "Then what the deuce do they mean by taking a postal man who is not even a postman?And if your husband had to go on deputation why on earth didn't he choose the Doordarshan instead?"

"I don't suppose he had any say in the matter," I said meekly. "Anyway, I don't see how his being in the Doordarshan could help you!" It was the time when Doordarshan ruled supreme and there was no Cable Television in India.

"At least he could have carried this letter personally then," said Mrs V, waving the envelope once again. "It contains photographs of my daughter and I simply daren't post them."

"Send them by registered post," I suggested.

"As if that would help!" scoffed Mrs V. "The postman would just grab my photos and reach the empty envelopes!That's what happens every time!I sent a whole pile of photos to Doordarshan last week and they never reached!"

"How do you know they didn't?" I asked curiously.

"Don't be silly," said Mrs V in an exasperated tone. "Had they reached, my daughter would be doing the announcements and the comparing and the interviews and not Sadhana, Mukta, Jyotsna and all that lot!"

"Why not reach your photos personally?" I asked. "That would be the simplest solution!"

Mrs V looked at me scathingly. "I can't think how you are a writer when you have so little imagination! You don't think I'm going to make her look common, do you? The Station Director should gasp as the photos tumble out of the envelope and then send for her. I won't have him telling me, "Ah, you have brought her photos, have you – as though she is after a clerical job!"

"Do the clerks in Doordarshan have to send their photos?" I asked.

"Please don't ask stupid questions," said Mrs. V frowning.

"Leave the packet with me, then" I said, getting tired of it all, "I'm going to Akashvani today. I'll step over at Doordarshan and reach it."

"No fears. You'd leave it in the bus. No, I'll have to post it after all and my daughter will have to face yet another heartbreak because of the dire dishonesty of your husband's department!"

"It isn't his department at the moment" I said.

"My dear," said Mrs V in a lofty voice, "You don't expect me to call a bee a butterfly just because he had deserted the hive for a while, do you?"

When Bobo Piped Up

"MUMMY, did you know that Mala's dad and Ritu's dad are bachelors?" said my younger daughter, dashing into the room. I choked over my tea, spilling half of it. "Don't say such things, Bobo" I cried aghast.

"But they **are,**" said Bobo cutting me short, "And why shouldn't I say it?"

"She means batch-mates, mama," said Chumki, my elder daughter. "Don't you, Bobo?"

"Yes," said Bobo, simply. "It was a slit of the tongue!"

"Slip, silly," said Chumki.

"It's what I meant," said Bobo.

Bobo has been a little Mrs. Malaprop from the word go. Not because she does not know the right words but because she fails to understand why two words which sound somewhat similar can't take the place of each other.

Once an old teacher of mine came to look me up and sat chatting with Chumki and Bobo. "Have they told you the story of the Bible in your school, dear?" she asked them. "Oh yes," said Bobo at once. "Teacher told us the story of the three kings who brought gold, mirch and a frank insect for the Baby Jesus."

"But that isn't correct, dear," said my teacher in a faint voice. "I know it isn't," said Bobo, "Babies don't eat chillies and I can't think why they brought an insect either!" My teacher was speechless with shock and I hastily introduced a safer subject. It was quite impossible for us to guess what Bobo would say next and to whom.

"I've asked the Maliks to dinner tomorrow," said my husband one evening. "For goodness's sake, see that Bobo doesn't come out with one of her outlandish remarks!"

The Maliks were the most starchy and straight-laced people imaginable and they did NOT have a sense of humour. "None of you girls are to speak a word unless spoken to," I told my daughters firmly. "Is that clear?"

"Yes, mama," they said obediently. I heaved a sigh of relief. True to their promise, they sat like a pair of dummies, answering questions with a bare yes or no.

The meal was nearly over when a heated discussion arose with everyone speaking nineteen to the dozen. Bobo fidgeted about in her chair for a while and said. "Shall I fetch the family-planning pack now, mama? It's in the fridge"

My husband coughed. I blushed. The chief guest frowned while the rest tittered. "What have you got in your fridge, eh?" asked one of the other guests with a wink.

I looked about me helplessly. Chumki came to the rescue as usual. "She means the ice-cream brick, mama. The shopkeeper calls it the family pack."

Bobo stood up, very much on her dignity. "What's wrong if I call it the family planning pack?" she asked. "Isn't the family planning to eat it for dinner?"

And .... That Is Life!

English and I

THE editor looked me up and down and asked, "Tell me, are these your first attempts at writing?"

"No sir," I stammered, handing him some of my books.He looked at the names of the publishers and shook his head. "Unstable," he said in a disapproving voice. "Authors who flit from one publisher to another are unreliable and ungrateful".

I tried to think of the perfect squelch but failed.And in any case, he had not yet done speaking. "Authors should never be so fickle," he added.

He then gave my stories a casual glance."Your English is rather below the mark," he remarked.I turned as purple as I could.Though I had prepared myself for the outright rejection of my plots I had certainly not expected an attack on the language of the stories.

He picked up the first story. "Look at this story, *The Clever Dog*.Now, Rani is obviously a female, so the story should have been called *The Clever Bitch*.In your next story you have said, 'Raju was a lovely baby'.A male child is a baba, not a baby. And you have called Tara a sweeper when she is evidently a sweeperess. Her mistress is a teacheress, not a teacher. You can't make mistakes in gender when you are writing for children."

He pounced upon the next story. "Take this line – 'He could not look her in the face.' Appalling! You don't **look** someone, you **look at** someone. You should have said, 'He could not look at her in the face'."

"But that is an idiom," I protested. He glared at me. "Idiom or not, it should be correct grammatically."

He read on in silence for a while. I was beginning to feel somewhat more hopeful. "Ah," he said, "See this line. 'I had put my foot in and no mistake'. Here is an error of omission. You ought to have mentioned the hole in the floor first. Otherwise how could he put a foot in?" He turned to another line. "Look at this, 'We really let our hair down'. Here is a sweeping generalization. Most girls have short hair these days and cannot possibly let it down."

The list of my shortcomings grew longer and longer. I rose at last. He nodded in obvious relief. "I am sorry I cannot accept your stories," he said, trying to sound kind, "But you see, I am a perfectionist."

"But words like baba, sweeperess, teacheress, co-brother-in-law are not English," I said. After all, I had nothing to lose! "You won't find them in the English dictionary!"

"Madam," he said, giving me an icy glare, "Just because the English dictionary has been careless in the matter, is there any reason why I should be?"

M for Milk!

"Gosh! We've left out list of vocabulary behind, exclaimed my friend as we stood outside the door of a huge departmental store.It was late and we were tired after a long day of lectures followed by a longer round of window-shopping.It was our first night in Tokyo and we were here to buy the bare necessities for our breakfast the next morning. This was Tokyo of 1986 when very few people in Japan spoke English. The Asian Centre for UNESCO (ACCU) where we had come as delegates to attend a month-long course in children's book production had warned us not to wander around alone unless we had someone to help us mainly because of the language problem. However, this 24-hour shop was right next door so there was no chance of our getting lost.

"Don't worry," I said with confidence, "They are sure to know the English for things like tea, milk and sugar." "I hope so", said my friend Flora in a doubtful voice, "I don't want to go back to the hotel empty-handed". We stepped in and exclaimed joyfully at the colourful display that met our eyes.We soon found the tea, sugar, bread, butter and biscuits.But NOT the milk.No amount of peeping, probing, shifting or searching helped us to discover just where it was kept.And the salesmen had no idea what we were looking for.

"I told you so!" said Flora in a disgusted voice.She was from Sri Lanka and cared about tea even more than I did. "We'll make them understand somehow," I said with rash confidence, "After all, what's sign-language for?They are bound to have milk-powder or at least condensed milk."

I had obviously over-estimated my histrionic abilities.No amount of miming on my part enabled them to understand what I was after.They took us to cupboards full of fruit-juice, syrups and squashes.And another chock-full of tea, coffee, cocoa and malts of various kinds.And finally to one that held cans of beer. "I can't imagine why they can't understand such a simple thing," I said, feeling harassed and embarrassed at the same time, as there was quite an audience by now, watching me with broad grins. "I suppose we'll have to have black tea tomorrow," said Flora in a gloomy voice. "Don't worry, it won't come to that," I said, making some more signs.

At last the salesman threw me a smile of comprehension and pointed to a shop across the street. "Come on, said Flora, "Perhaps it's a dairy".We thanked the salesman – using the only Japanese phrase we'd picked up – and dashed across the street to the other shop.

A sleepy salesman sat dozing by the encounter.I repeated the signs.The salesman smiled and pointed to the shelves all round.They were stacked with whiskey, brandy, rum and what have you.It was an exclusive liquor-shop! "Well…er…," I stammered, not knowing what to say. "Look, there's another departmental shop over there," said Flora, "Let's try our luck for the last time.Incidentally, you ought to have made signs to show a baby.That would have made them understand". "You'd better go in first," I said.Flora rocked her arms to show a baby – crooning for milk.The salesman smiled, nodded and vanished inside another room to return triumphantly with a …FEEDING BOTTLE!

Mother-in-law's pals

WE saw them day after day.A tall man with a woman on either side.Clinging to each other through thick and thin, through the bustle and din of the crowded city.Tokyo was a-stir with conventions and seminars that fortnight.The trio was attending one such event just as we were.As we put up in the same hotel and our venues were in the same locality, we constantly bumped into one another – in lifts and lobbies, shops and subways and of course, the metro.

"Why do those three stick together like that?" asked Flora from Sri Lanka. "Perhaps both women are in love with him," said Jana from Indonesia.She was to be married shortly and saw everything through a romantic haze.The rest of us hooted with laughter. The trio hardly looked lover-like! "I guess they are live-in friends," said Irene from the Philippines. "Oh no! Not those three! They don't look fast enough for that sort of thing," said Farishte from Iran, sounding positively horrified. More laughter followed. "Well, WHY is he chasing the two women then?" demanded Yi from Korea.

"Is he chasing them?" I asked thoughtfully, "He doesn't seem energetic enough somehow." "Let's make friends with them," said Flora, "Then we'll know for sure."

But the trio was NOT interested in making friends with us and simply looked the other way after a brief nod. But Flora wasn't going to give up so easily. She ran after them, saying, "My friends and I would like to know you. We are... "UNESCO delegates," said one of the dames, peering through her glasses. "Attending the ACCU workshop," said the man. "Good Day," said the second dame and all three walked away briskly. "Well I never!" said Flora indignantly. "We told you so!" cried the rest of us.

But we couldn't get the trio out of our minds.

"Perhaps they work in the same office and he is their boss," said Irene.

"So they are trying to remain in his good books," added Yi.

"He doesn't look old enough to be their boss," said Flora.

"Then he must be a prospective bridegroom, engaged to the relative of one of the dames," said Jana.

"Then why hang on to the other dame as well?" asked Farishte. "He can't be engaged to a relative of both!"

One absurd speculation followed another and the topic soon became a source of entertainment for us.

Then one evening we saw them buying meat and vegetables. "See that?" said Flora. "The dames are having a party for him!" "Lucky chap!" said the rest of us. There was a shout of laughter from a new friend who had joined our group the previous night. "It's lucky dames, if you ask me," she said.

"Do you know them?" I asked eagerly. "As it happens, I do," she said. "Those two ladies loathe cooking. The chap offered to cook for all three the first day. Out of sheer politeness, you know. And they haven't let him out of their clutches ever since! He can't even refuse, poor fellow! They're pals of his mother-in-law, you see!"

My Husband's Director

Not all writers are absent-minded. But those who **are**, sometimes get into the most absurd scrapes because their heads are stuck in the clouds at the wrong moment. This is what happened to me when my husband was posted in a small town. My neighbors plainly disapproved of me because I was always reading or scribbling instead of dusting, cooking or sewing. Nevertheless, they dropped in now and then with the hope of getting me interested in the more important things of life.

I usually dreaded their visits. But that evening I welcomed them enthusiastically because I had something to say that would interest them.

"Have you been out?" asked the first lady, looking at my travelling-case.

"Yes," I replied with a broad smile, "I've just returned from Chitrakoot."

I could feel the warmth of approval in the air. Chitrakoot was a much sought after place of pilgrimage.
"Did your husband take you?" asked the second lady.
"No, he had an important meeting," I replied, "I went with his Director."

I saw them exchange glances and shrugged. I couldn't help it if my husband happened to be a workaholic!And I couldn't expect him to miss office to take me anywhere, let alone a holy place.

"I suppose his director also took his family?" asked the third lady.

"Oh no," I said, thinking of the Mandakini River and the limpid, green pools among the rocks, "We didn't want the children to miss school. I didn't take mine either."

There was a pause. "Isn't it a rather long journey?" asked the first lady giving me a queer look, "You must have returned well past midnight!"

"Oh, we stayed the night there and visited the temples and caves the next morning," I replied and added, "One can't enjoy the gorgeous scenery if one is in a hurry."

I was thinking of the long road to Chitrakoot with flocks of peacocks and deer roaming wild part of the way.

"It's lucky you found rooms at such short notice," said the second lady in a strange voice. "Yes indeed," I replied, "The place was teeming with people. I didn't think we'd get a room either and both of us were so thankful when we did."

I am not observant by nature. But even I could feel the icy tang in the air. The silence that followed was so solid, you could have cut it with a knife! I was even more astonished when they refused tea and rose abruptly after what seemed an incredulously shorttime. I supposed it was because I gushed about the beauty of the place rather than its religious significance. And then I suddenly realized that I had not bothered to spell out yet another significant fact: My husband's director, with whom I shared a room at Chitrakoot, was a lady!

Just Walking in the Rain

Last night's rain brought back an old memory of another rainy day way back in 1981 when my daughters were in middle and primary school. My husband was posted in Indore which was a green and sylvan town in those days, with wide open green meadows. I had three other friends who were also my neighbours and our children attended the same school, leaving around 9 in the morning and returning home around 4 in the evening. Four of us often went for the afternoon cinema show, our chief entertainment during those days. The show started at 12 and was over by 3 pm so we always reached home long before the children and had ample time to prepare their tea.

One afternoon as we stepped out of the cinema hall we found that it was raining cats and dogs. None of us were carrying umbrellas as it was merely cloudy when we had left home. We realized that we simply had to get back before the children returned from school, rain or no rain! We had to cross an open meadow to reach the main road and as we stepped out gingerly we were soon drenched to the skin. It was raining so hard that we could barely see the way ahead. Just then a little urchin came running and stopped us, saying, *amma* was calling us. We turned back and saw a little tin shed with plastic curtains and a roof made of asbestos sheets in the middle of the meadow. A lady stood at the door calling us loudly and urgently. Almost instinctively we made for the shed and the lady literally pulled us inside, scolding us loudly in Sindhi.

I blinked in wonder as I looked about me. The place was not just neat and tidy but also spotlessly clean. The lady called her *bahus* (daughters-in-law) who stood nearby, ordering one to fetch towels and the other to make cups of *adrakh ki chai* (ginger tea) immediately. We gazed surprised as the bahu pulled out a steel trunk and took out four brand new towels and handed them to us. The lady ordered us to dry ourselves immediately while the second bahu got us piping hot tea in gleaming steel glasses. As we sipped the tea the lady told us that we should not have tried to go out in such rain and should never do it again. We nodded meekly. She told us proudly that her two sons were truck drivers who plied between Indore and Bombay and that there was 'no lack of anything' in her house although she lived in a shed made of tin sheets. We thanked her and started for home as it had stopped raining by then. Obviously it had been a brief cloudburst.

I wondered last night if anyone would go off to a total stranger's place today without giving it a second thought, as we had done. More importantly, would anyone care if four totally unknown and unrelated strangers got drenched in the rain?

The Celebration

Speaking of Indore made me remember another amazing incident.

There used to be a 10-day-long celebration during Ganesh puja where people of the entire locality took part. A stage was set up next to the Ganesh idol and every evening there was something – music, dance, skits, story-telling et al – for which everyone turned up. Most of the cultural programmes were done by the children but the housewives were roped in on the last day, either to sing a song or tell a joke or an anecdote. A few young housewives opted to dance and weregracefully included in the general programme.A group of young boys who were in charge went from house to house, took down names and simply would not take 'no' for an answer. So there we all were – some singing in tune, some out of tune, the words going haywire in most cases! It was all part of the fun.

During my second year the boys brought a list of 'evergreen' songs and asked us to tick the ones we knew. "We want a change this time. Last year 11 aunties sang *diwanahuabadal*, 13 aunties sang *babujidhirechalna* and 10 aunties sang *gaatarahemera dil*. And we could do nothing! This time **we** are going to choose the songs. We'll ask some uncles to join in too.""That's good", I said, not dreaming what lay in store for me!

The programme went with a swing with no song being repeated until I heard the announcement, "We shall now have the *sadabahar* (evergreen) duet *aajasanammadhurchandnimein hum* presented by Sm. Swapna Dutta and Sri Anant Saxena. My heart skipped a beat, for not only had we never practiced the song together even once, but I didn't know the said gentleman from Adam! I was equally sure that he did not have the ghost of an idea as to who I was, either! Anyway, we were being called on the stage and I got up looking dazed at the sea of faces before me. The gentleman followed me and asked, *aapko words yaadhainna? kyon ki mujheyaadnahinhain* (do you remember the words of the song? Because I don't). I nodded. There was a ripple of laughter as the mike was switched on already and the audience could hear him clearly.

He started the song. I followed. He kept singing my lines by mistake so I had to sing his! Then he suddenly stopped and said, *awazshayadzyadaunchahai, thodaneecheletahoon*(I think the notes are too high, I'll go a scale lower). I was quite sure that I sounded like a screeching owl so I merely nodded once again. Since no one remembered who was supposed to sing which line of the last verse, we sang it in tandem and somehow managed to complete the song.*kam se kambesura to nahingaya* (at least we didn't sing out of tune), he said triumphantly and jumped down from the stage. I didn't know whether the clapping that followed was for the song or the strange situation but at least we had managed to entertain the crowd! After I went home my 6-year-old daughter asked, "Mama, what was the song you sang with Raju's *taoji* (uncle)?" The said Raju must obviously be one of her playmates, I realized.Goodness! So is that *who* he was??

I am quite sure no one can imagine such a situation today!

Pirate Books

I wonder how many of you have come across a pirate edition of some timeless classic. When my mother said that she was longing to read "Gone With The Wind" once again I hastily picked up a copy from the pavement that had a beautiful cover. I was leaving for the station in a few hours' time and had no time to visit a bookshop. My mother was delighted with the gift. She took the book from me and opened a page at random.... and frowned. The first line read: *Rhett Butler said, "Scarlet, remove the semi-colon; replace with coma.."*

The pirate edition had printed the editorial comments along with the text! And the entire book was replete with such lines! I went to a bookshop that very evening and bought her a fresh copy of Gone With The Wind although it did not have a flashy cover like the pirate one!

Durga Puja When We Were Young

Mahalaya is over and we are into Navaratri and I am surprised to see how cool I am about it, as though I am a far off spectator. What I had not realized so strongly before is the fact that it is one's near and dear ones who give life, meaning and significance to a festival. When they are not there a festival day is like any other with just a little difference.

I remember how eagerly we waited - virtually counted the days - for the Durga Puja to arrive when I was young. One main reason was because the puja was held in our house with my grandfather playing the pivotal role and we - my sister and I - watched it from the very first stage when the image of the goddess was constructed, stage by stage, in the *dalan* (covered veranda) where the puja was finally performed. Durga puja had been performed in Dadu's (my grandfather's) family for generations and Dadu continued the tradition wherever he was.

My first memories of the puja being performed in Patna where Dadu was last posted during his service period are somewhat vague. But one scene is etched in my memory - that of the whole family going out in a boat for the *visarjan* (immersion) and finally Dadu and Chordadu (his younger brother) jumping into the river holding the image of the goddess from both sides. Both were strong swimmers and climbed back into the boat once again after the goddess was safely immersed in the Ganges.

What I really remember vividly are the pujas held in Dadu'sHazaribagh house after his retirement. My sister and I were in school by then (she was in the nursery, and I in middle/high school). Two brothers - Mahadev and Sahadev - made the image in the puja dalan(closed veranda) . First the basic structure in straw and then with three separate coatings of mud. When it was fully dry the image was whitened with liquid chalk and then, finally, came the colours. My sister and I threw off our school bags and rushed to the dalan to watch them goggle-eyed the moment we were back from school and refused to budge until the brothers left. Mamoi (my grandmother) would get busy well before a month rolling up wicks from white cotton cloth, cooking the coconut laddos and mawa sweets that would be needed in enormous quantities, with all of us - including many ladies from our neighbourhood - helping her.

But what we looked forward to most of all was the arrival of the rest of the family. Ma and Baba came before anyone else and then Mashimoni (my aunt) and Meshomasai (uncle) with our cousins, Dipudi and Khokanda. And lastly Chordadu came with his whole family (no matter where he was posted) on *Panchami* (5th day of the Navaratri or Durga puja) day as he could not leave his work earlier than that. There were ear-marked rooms for Chordadu and Chordidi, Mashimoni and Meshomasai, the rest of us fitting in where we could.

With Chordadu came our young uncles and aunts - Tublumashi, Bablumama, Tultulmashi, Chulbul and Kumkum. It was the arrival of the family that set off the actual festive season. Ma, Tublumashi , Dipudi, Khokanda and Bablumama took charge of the *alpana* (floor painting) and general decorations, with the rest of us helping. Tultulmashi and Chulbul were very good at alpana too. Chordadu was a good artist and he always painted the eyes of the goddesses, Durga, Lakshmi and Saraswati. So the image was left incomplete until Chordadu arrived and painted the eyes.

What fun it was, helping in the puja preparations every day! We, the youngsters were asked to get the choicest flowers from the garden, pick out the *durba* grass and collect the *bel* leaves that would be needed in enormous quantities. Attending the varied rituals of the puja – picking out the *Kala-bou* from dadu's banana grove, the *maha-snan* (ritualistic bathing of the goddess) and finally the *pushpanjali* (offering of flowers) for which Dadu himself read out the mantras. And of course, the *arati* where we ourselves beat the drum and the *kansar* (metal drum).

Frying puris for the prasad was yet another excitement. I remember it was Bablumama who taught Tultulmashi and me how to fry puris. How joyful the entire experience was just cannot be described in words. I remember the enormous durry spread out in the hall with mattresses and pillows and how all the young crowd slept there, talking and joking well into the midnight. And so it continued right up to the Lakshmi Puja after which tearful goodbyes would begin and the house would be quiet once again.

I remember enjoying the pujas once again as a family - with my husband and daughters - at Indore and Delhi where all of us were happily involved, especially when we were in Saket. But now, with both daughters away, the pujas hardly seem like a festival. We still visit the goddess and offer *pushpanjali* but the spirit of festivity seems to have disappeared for good.

A Long Power Cut

Yesterday we had a power cut of nearly 10 hours at a stretch in the evening. Despite having an inverter, we were too scared to make use of it not knowing whether the power would return during the night or not.

As I sat on the balcony looking at the sea of darkness all around I remembered my early childhood days in Hazaribagh when there was no electricity. Even my first year or two in school was during that period. Strange to think that we never even missed it! On the contrary, the very ritual of seeing the elders light the hurricanes (lanterns) and my grandpa light the huge petromax every evening was exciting. It was fun carrying a lantern when moving about and seeing the strange shadows on the walls. Hazaribagh was deliciously cool even at the peak of summer, hemmed in with lush green trees all around. It was fun sleeping on the terrace which was the coolest after sundown and falling asleep watching the stars above. During my brief period in the school hostel I remember four of us had to share a table lamp while doing our home-work. I remember the first Parents' Day function in school where there was a Punch-and-Judy show where they sang:

"Do you know the plans of D.V.C?

Electric lights we are going to see!"

The song was composed by Rev. Mother Vera. She taught us the song in one of the music classes. We loved the song and continued to sing it long after the advent of electricity. How strange it seems now! Life was so simple and people were not unduly disturbed even by such a basic need as electricity!

Hand-me-down Books

I am sure today's youngsters would be thunderstruck if I were to tell them that when we were in school there was no concept of new books being prescribed every year for basic subjects. Right from my mother and dad's time there were "standard" textbooks for maths, at least in Eastern India.

Geometry meant the book by Hall & Stevens; Algebra meant a textbook by K.P. Basu; Arithmetic meant another textbook by Jadab Chakrabarty and the most popular Trigonometry book was by Forester & Mitra.

So, as soon as I reached middle school I inherited my mother's Hall & Stevens (Books 1-6, bound together) and Basu's Algebra and my dad's Jadab Chakrabarty and also his Forester & Mitra. Similarly, I was given my mother's Nesfield's Grammar (Books 1-4) and also her Wren & Martin. I used all these books right from middle school up to high school. After me, my sister who is 8 years younger than I am, used them all. That is how textbooks became "family" books, to be passed on from the elder to the younger members of the family, from one generation to the next.

My parents must have lost their geography textbooks (or else, they didn't read them at that stage). Soon after reaching high school Mr. Rathore, who was a visiting teacher in our school, took us for geography. He asked us to buy a book by L.Dudley Stamp, which, he said we could use right up to our final year in school. It turned out to be another delightful book, full of facts, lucidly and delightfully told. It was another of my favourite books in school which was really very useful.

Do the students have books now which can safely take them along their entire period of high school? Or perhaps the concept itself is too old fashioned to be considered? But when I read the newspaper every morning I fervently wish that some of the sub-editors (??) had read Nesfield or Wren & Martin's Grammar during their school days! At least then they would have some idea about which prepositions to use!

How Much is Too Much?

As I stepped inside the Calcutta airport yesterday afternoon, I heard strains of a melodious guitar (played only as Sunil Ganguly can) playing my all-time favourite pieces - *zindagi ka safar, tere mere sapne, diwanahuabaadal, ye jeevanhai* et al.

I listened entranced the first time... charmed, the second time... delighted the third time... jittery the fourth time ... annoyed the fifth time (why don't they play another CD by him, for God's sake?).. exasperated the sixth time (has the system got stuck or something?),... annoyed the seventh time (why doesn't someone tell them??) and hopping mad the eighth time and thereafter! They played the same track over and over again for 2 hours (Our airline had sent an SMS asking the passengers to report 2 hours prior to the flight) until we finally took off!

MORAL: one **CAN** have too much of a good thing!!!

A question of marketing

As I went out for my usual morning walk in the park this morning I recalled my first year in Bangalore, a new city for me, nearly 14 years ago. I had been visiting a bookshop when a young girl walked up to me and asked me if I was new to the city and how I liked it. We got chatting about this and that and she seemed very friendly. I was impressed by her cordial behaviour, more so, when she asked me if she could look me up when she came to my locality and asked for my address.

She landed up the very next day. I was having my mid-morning tea and asked her to join me. After a few sips she said, "you know, Aunty, I am really involved in a project and would like to tell you about it."

"A project...?" I asked.

"It's about some fantastic products, "she said.

I instantly knew what was coming! I had already met quite a few like her in Delhi. The only difference was that they did not wait for a full day before broaching the subject.

"If you are talking about XYZ products, please save your breath," I said, "Because I am not interested."
She looked like an inflated balloon and then I noticed her bulging bag which held some of the products.
"It's not that I mind people selling their ware but I prefer a direct approach rather than all this beating about the bush," I said.

"Are you quite sure you don't want to try some of these?" she asked me, "They are fantastic! And if you join our team it is a sure and easy way of making money."
"As I've just told you, I am not interested," I said.
She left abruptly without even saying goodbye.

Soon afterwards our park was invaded by a group of smart, well dressed youngsters who tried to catch hold of the walkers, mostly ladies, and get them to join their "movement" of making easy money. Some fell for it. Some did not. Then they got some of their 'leaders' to give the interested people a pep talk. I looked on with some amusement. The ladies who got involved told me that they had a unique method of catching clients.

"How?" I asked.

"Well," said the lady, "They have been training us for the last few weeks how to get hold of prospective clients without their suspecting what exactly we want from them!"

Things change with time! Marketing techniques must have changed too, over the years, I told myself. Although I could walk fast even a few years ago I was virtually limping now because of my bad knee. Suddenly a stranger stopped me and suggested what I could do to relieve the pain in my knee and what would help.

"That's really nice of you," I said gratefully. "Then, there's a special pain balm that is far better than any in the market, "she added, "Also some juices which make the pain virtually vanish."

"Ah!" I thought, this sounds familiar!

"I could get you the products," she said, "And reach them at your place".

"Are you talking about XYZ?" I asked, amused. "Oh no. They are a big fraud! Mine are by ABC," she said.

Who says marketing techniques change???

Unspoken goodbye

It was one of those "telephone friendships" that crop up all of a sudden. I had always liked Modhumita Mojumdar's regular columns in newspapers, mainly because she often wrote about children's literature and Bengali literature – two subjects close to my heart. When she reviewed my Juneli books in The Statesman I decided to call her up and thank her. We had a friend in common from whom I got her phone number. Apparently she too had been trying to get in touch with me for some information on women's magazines in Bengali.

After that first phone call we called each other off and on, usually to discuss new books, plays or films, and sometimes, just random thoughts. Gradually we grew familiar with each other's voices and views despite the fact that we had never met and neither knew what the other looked like! And we knew very little about each other's personal life. I knew she had a daughter who was working and she knew that I had two, both in school. But that was about it. We often planned to meet up but somehow it never materialized because of our respective commitments and schedules.

Some months later The Book Review asked me to edit a special Bengali number that they were planning to bring out. I thought Modhumita would be the right person to review Taslima Nasreen's "Nirbachito Column" which had been creating ripples. When I called her up an unknown voice told me that Modhumita was in hospital for a major surgery. The line went dead before I could ask anything more and I wondered what was wrong. She hadn't mentioned anything when I spoke to her barely two days ago! I was even more surprised when she called me three days later.

"I thought you were in hospital," I said surprised.

"I was. I'm home now. I heard you had called," she said.

I asked her how she was but she evaded my question and asked, "Why did you call me? Any particular reason?"

I told her why and added that she need not give it a thought until she was better. Modhumita just laughed. "Being in bed won't stop me from writing. Besides, I liked that book."

Despite her illness hers was the very first review that I received. Whenever I asked her how she was she assured me that her little problems were nothing to write home about and went on to speak of something else. I didn't suggest looking her up because I felt that she would rather be alone. But she sounded decidedly under the weather when I spoke to her next.

"What's up? Haven't you recovered as yet?" I asked.

"Not quite, perhaps," she replied, sounding totally unlike herself.

"Take a break, for goodness' sake, and don't overdo things," I urged.

"How can I?" she replied with her usual trill of laughter, "Writing happens to be my bread and butter."

"Then write in bed," I said.

"But I am not a creative writer," she remarked, "My writing is mostly first hand report of things. So I've got to be up and about. Tell you what, lunch with me at the Press Club this Saturday. We really must meet, you know.""Yes, it's about time we did," I said and promised to turn up no matter what happened.

But our Saturday tryst never materialized. I read in the papers that Friday that Modhumita was no more. She had passed away quietly the night before. I never got the chance to see her. Not even to say good bye!

Yesterday Once More

WHEN I think of the happiest period of my life, my thoughts invariably hover around College Street.Not the College Street of today's Kolkata but that delightful haven of yesteryears where books used to be spread out and stacked up on the pavements in a delightfully unorthodox manner.Here, along the railings of the Presidency College Shakespeare brushed shoulders with Cheiro and Bernard Shaw reposed peacefully between the portly pages of *Subarnalata* and *Kori DiyeKinlaam*. Karl Marx lay complacently sandwiched between Perry Mason and *Raghuvangsham* while Hall and Stevens stood cheek by jowl with *Kamasutra*.

No one minded our browsing amongst them for hours on end.And then, popping into the Coffee House for a refreshing glass of cold coffee.College Street and the Coffee House are the two places where memories hang thick and I always long for another look at the one-time Mecca of our student days.

But the jolt which I received when I stepped there after a long, long absence was not altogether pleasant.The books were no longer spread out at random.I couldn't even touch them without telling the owner of the "shoplet" (where the books now reposed) what exactly I had in mind!There were no merry groups hovering around; none of the chaff and banter which used to be an integral part of our pavement culture in bygone days.

I wondered whether the Coffee House too had changed beyond recognition.Fortunately the old familiar aroma of coffee mixed with Charminar (a popular brand of cheaper cigarette) wafted up my nostrils as I climbed up the stairs.The place was full of young people – far more sophisticated than we ever were, no doubt, – sitting in cosy groups just the way we did. The hall was not jam-packed and I could easily make my way to the corner table where my friend Krishna and I always sat.By the time I ordered my coffee I was 18 once again, seeing everything as it used to be then!

I smiled as I remembered the right-hand corner table where Manoj whiled away impatient hours, waiting for Suravi. I could almost see all the other starry-eyed duos - Sidhu and Indrani, Gautam and Indu, Mihir and Malini, Bill and Dipali and many others who might have popped the question at this very spot!I recalled how we had gorged on "Kashmiri chicken" (the most expensive item on the Coffee House menu-card those days) when Sujit gave us a treat on getting his first job-and nearly had him broke;How Anurita made eyes at all and sundry and how Tirthankar used to startle us with his loud and sudden hoots of laughter.Where were they now?

Then my eyes fell on another special table.It was always occupied by Saumitra Chatterjee and his group around 11 A.M. I vividly recalled his sitting there, looking devastatingly handsome in his ash-coloured kurta, and how Indrani (after laying a bet with us) had walked up to him to say hello.Three of his films were being released that afternoon and he had calmly advised her against seeing any of them as they were all "trash"!

I suddenly discovered some of the youngsters looking at me curiously.I was sure they were wondering what a staid old matron like myself was doing in a young people's joint!I didn't belong there anymore!Not after all these years!Memories might play strange tricks but they didn't really count!Just then the waiter came up with the bill.He flashed me a smile of recognition.He was grey now but I remembered him too!That smile brought back my lost yesterday-assuring me that here at least was a corner where time stood still!

About the Author

Swapna Dutta has been writing books for children for nearly five decades with over 50 titles to her credit, including translations, published by Hachette, Orient Blackswan, Scholastic, Shristi, Children's Book Trust, National Book Trust, Pan Macmillan and others. Two of her books have been listed by White Ravens (International Youth Library, Munich) and 32 in Good Reads. Her contribution to magazines includes Children's World, Target, The Bookbird (USA), Cricket (USA), The School Magazine (Australia), Scottish Home & Country (UK) and Folly (UK). She worked as Editorial Consultant with Target (Living Media), Assistant Editor, Limca Book of Records; and Deputy Editor, Encyclopaedia Britannica, India, between 1988 and 2002. Dutta has presented papers on various aspects of children's literature at national and international conferences (including IBBY) and has won several prizes and awards for her work and a National Fellowship from the Ministry of Culture.

www.ingramcontent.com/pod-product-compliance
Lightning Source LLC
LaVergne TN
LVHW041537070526
838199LV00046B/1714